This Little Tiger book belongs to:

_____

_____

_____

To my very own
'Scrap', Lorcan
— MO

LITTLE TIGER PRESS
1 The Coda Centre, 189 Munster Road, London SW6 6AW
www.littletiger.co.uk

First published in Great Britain 2005
This edition published 2016

Text and illustrations copyright © Mark Oliver 2005
Mark Oliver has asserted his right to be identified as the author
and illustrator of this work under the Copyright,
Designs and Patents Act, 1988

A CIP catalogue record for this book is available from the British Library

Printed in China • LTP/1900/1407/1215

2 4 6 8 10 9 7 5 3 1

ROBOT DOG

MARK OLIVER

LITTLE TIGER PRESS
London

In a factory, on a hill,
a huge machine made
robot dogs.

The robot dogs rolled out of the factory and were delivered to owners who played with them and loved them and cared for them.

The dogs were very happy because all dogs, even robot dogs, want an owner.

One little dog on the conveyor belt was very excited.

"I wonder what my owner will be like," he said. "What will I be called?"

He was much too excited to sit still — he jumped and frolicked and bounced up and down. But then,

CRASH!

he bounced too high and clonked his ear. At once alarm bells rang, red lights flashed and a cloud of smoke whooshed as the huge machine ground slowly to a stop.

The machine inspected the robot dog very carefully. Finally a voice boomed:

"NOT RUSTY OR DUSTY,

NOT BATTERED OR BENT,

NO PATCHES OR SCRATCHES,

BUT THERE IS A DENT!

SCRAP!"

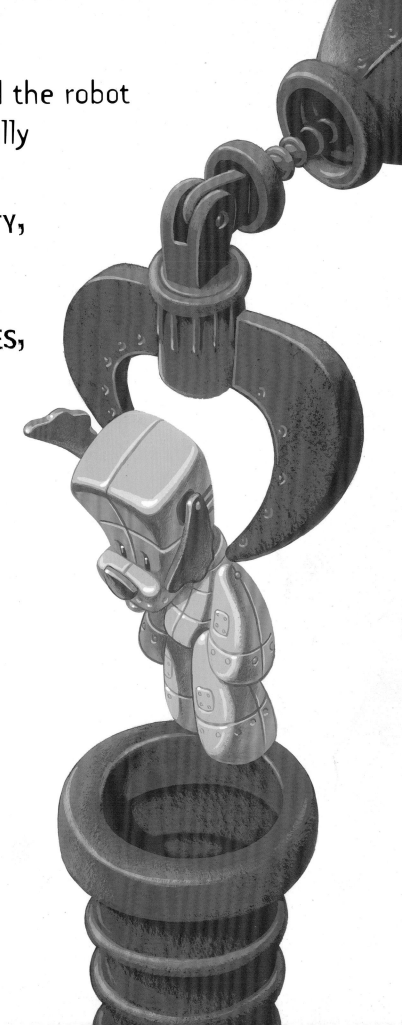

"So that's my name!" thought Scrap as the machine picked him up and dropped him through a hatch.

Scrap slid down a chute
and landed in a yard full of junk.
    There, staring at him, were
some other dogs.
    "Hello!" he said. "I'm Scrap!
Where am I? Where's my owner?"
    One of the dogs said, "You don't have
an owner — you're a reject like us."

Bumper, Dent, Scratch and Sniffer
all lived in the yard. They made
it comfortable and it was
a wonderful place to play,
just a bit messy, the
way dogs like it.

They often played with other
dogs who had owners.
But sooner or later their
owners would call:

"Come on, Shiny."
"Dinner time, Sparkle."

Then they stopped
whatever they were
doing and ran home.

Seeing the other dogs
go off happily to their
owners made the yard
dogs feel a bit sad.

"Why don't we get an owner?"
said Scrap one day.

"They take a lot of looking after," replied Bumper. "They like things to be tidy and you need to play games and fuss over them to keep them happy."

But the more they all talked about it, the more they *really* wanted an owner.

"How can we get one?" said Sniffer. "We're rejects!"

"There must be a way," thought Scrap.

As Scrap started thinking, the cogs in his brain started turning. They went round faster and faster as he thought harder and harder.

Finally a light flickered on!

"I've got an idea!" Scrap announced to the other dogs, excitedly. "Come and help me!"

The dogs raced round collecting
anything that might be useful.

They worked all day and all night and by the next morning the dogs were exhausted, but very proud, because . . .

. . . there stood an owner!

He was rusty and dusty, battered and
bent, patched, scratched and covered
in dents — but he had a heart of gold.

Their owner played with
them and loved them and
cared for them. And the dogs
were very happy, because all
dogs, even robot dogs,
want an owner.

#0000